TICO
and the Golden Wings

TICO
and the Golden Wings

Leo Lionni

Alfred A. Knopf

New York

Many years ago
I knew a little bird
whose name was Tico.
He would sit on my shoulder
and tell me all about the flowers,
the ferns, and the tall trees.
Once Tico told me
this story about himself.

I don't know how it happened,
but when I was young
I had no wings.
I sang like the other birds
and I hopped like them,
but I couldn't fly.

Luckily my friends loved me. They flew from tree to tree and in the evening they brought me berries and tender fruits gathered from the highest branches.

Often I asked myself, "Why can't I fly like the other birds? Why can't I, too, soar through the big blue sky over villages and treetops?"

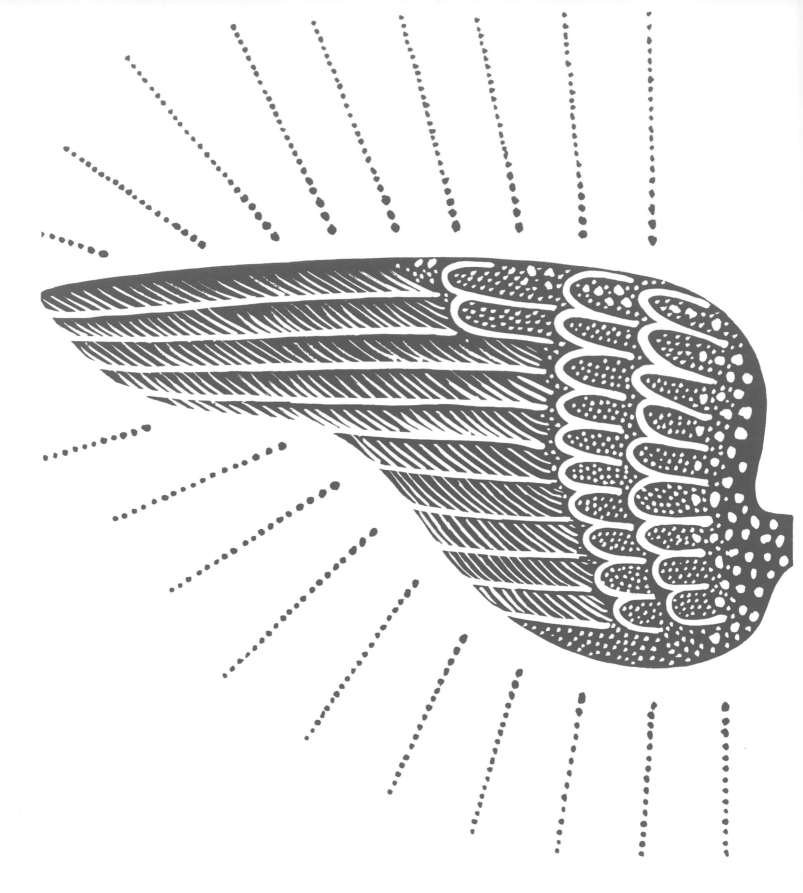

And I dreamt that I had golden wings, strong enough

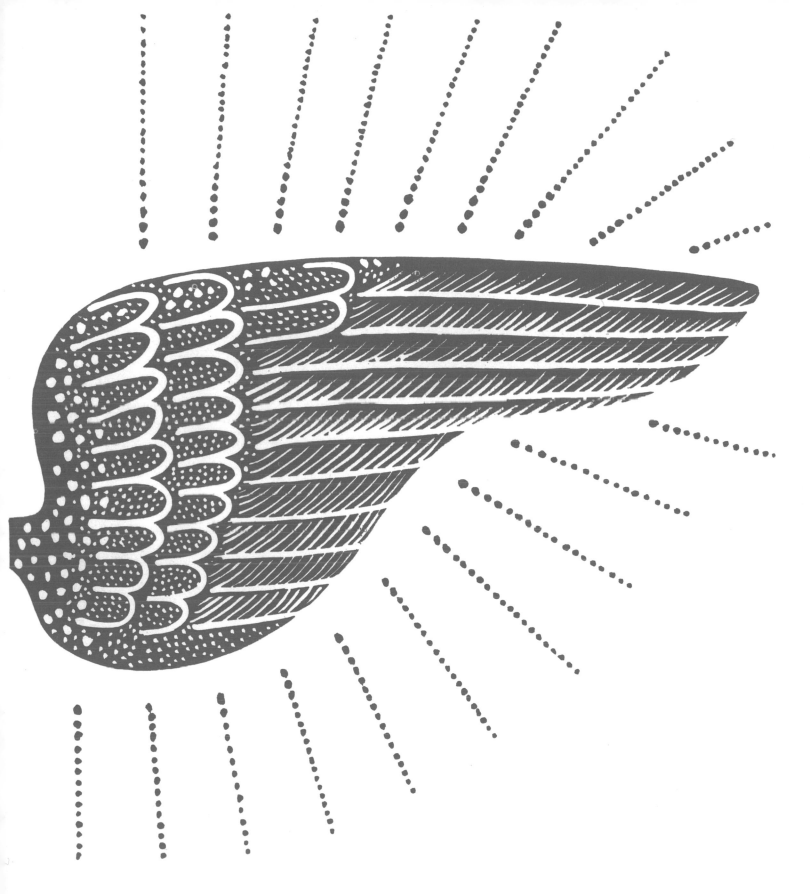

to carry me over the snowcapped mountains far away.

One summer night I was awakened by a noise nearby. A strange bird, pale as a pearl, was standing behind me.
"I am the wishingbird," he said. "Make a wish and it will come true."

I remembered my dreams and with all my might I wished I had a pair of golden wings. Suddenly there was a flash of light and on my back there were wings, golden wings, shimmering in the moonlight. The wishingbird had vanished.

Cautiously I flapped my wings. And then I flew.
I flew higher than the tallest tree. The flower patches below
looked like stamps scattered over the countryside
and the river like a silver necklace lying in the meadows.
I was happy and I flew well into the day.

But when my friends saw me
swoop down from the sky,
they frowned on me and said,
"You think you are better than we are,
don't you, with those golden wings.
You wanted to be *different*."
And off they flew
without saying another word.

Why had they gone? Why were they angry?
Was it *bad* to be different?
I could fly as high as the eagle.
Mine were the most beautiful wings in the world.
But my friends had left me and I was very lonely.

One day I saw a man sitting
in front of a hut.
He was a basketmaker
and there were baskets
all around him.
There were tears in his eyes.
I flew onto a branch from
where I could speak to him.

"Why are you sad?" I asked.
"Oh, little bird, my child is sick
and I am poor.
I cannot buy the medicines
that would make him well."
"How can I help him?" I thought.
And suddenly I knew.
"I will give him one of my feathers."

"How can I thank you!" said the poor man happily.
"You have saved my child. But look! Your wing!"
Where the golden feather had been
there was a real black feather, as soft as silk.

From that day, little by little,
I gave my golden feathers away
and black feathers appeared in their place.
I bought many presents:
three new puppets for a poor puppeteer . . .

a spinning wheel to spin the yarn for an old woman's shawl . . .

a compass for a fisherman who got lost at sea . . .

And when I had given my last golden feathers
to a beautiful bride,
my wings were as black as India ink.

I flew to the big tree
where my friends gathered for the night.
Would they welcome me?

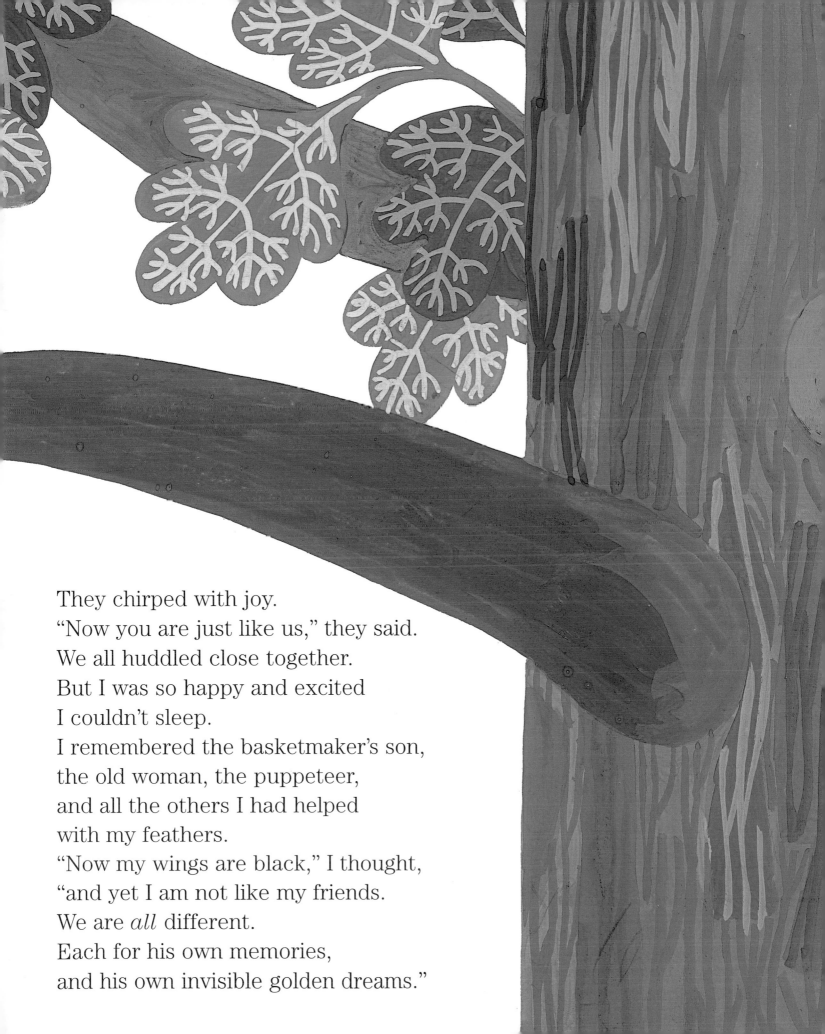

They chirped with joy.
"Now you are just like us," they said.
We all huddled close together.
But I was so happy and excited
I couldn't sleep.
I remembered the basketmaker's son,
the old woman, the puppeteer,
and all the others I had helped
with my feathers.
"Now my wings are black," I thought,
"and yet I am not like my friends.
We are *all* different.
Each for his own memories,
and his own invisible golden dreams."

THIS IS A BORZOI BOOK PUBLISHED BY ALFRED A. KNOPF

Published in the United States by Alfred A. Knopf, an imprint of Random House Children's Books,
a division of Random House, Inc., New York.

KNOPF, BORZOI BOOKS, and the colophon are registered trademarks of Random House, Inc.

www.randomhouse.com/kids

Educators and librarians, for a variety of teaching tools, visit us at www.randomhouse.com/teachers

This title was originally cataloged by the Library of Congress as follows:
Lionni, Leo.
Tico and the golden wings; illus. by the author.
SUMMARY: Illustrations and text tell about a bird without wings who is given golden wings by the wishing
bird. He loses his friends because they are envious. When he gives away his golden feathers, one by one,
to help others, he is given feathers like the other birds and they welcome him back.
1. Fairy tales. 2. Birds—Stories. I. Title
L.C. Catalog Card Number: 64-18321

ISBN 978-0-394-81749-1 (trade) — ISBN 978-0-394-91749-8 (lib. bdg.) — ISBN 978-0-394-83078-0 (pbk.)

MANUFACTURED IN MALAYSIA

10 9 8 7 6 5 4 3 2 1

Hardcover reissue September 2007